LEO AND EMILY'S ZOO

by FRANZ BRANDENBERG
pictures by YOSSI ABOLAFIA

Greenwillow Books · New York

Watercolors and a black pen line
were used for the full-color art.
The text type is ITC Usherwood.

First Edition   10 9 8 7 6 5 4 3 2 1

Library of Congress Cataloging-in-Publication Data

Brandenberg, Franz.
Leo and Emily's zoo.
Summary: When Leo and Emily decide to open
their own zoo and charge admission, they
encounter a few problems, but their families
find a unique way to turn disaster into success.
[1. Zoos—Fiction. 2. Moneymaking projects—Fiction]
I. Abolafia, Yossi, ill.   II. Title.
PZ7.B7364Lh   1988   [E]   87-14880
ISBN 0-688-07457-X
ISBN 0-688-07458-8 (lib. bdg.)

FOR PHILIP ANDRÉ

"I wish we could go to the zoo," said Leo.

"It's very expensive," said Emily.

"We could make our own zoo," said Leo.

"We'll charge ten cents admission," said
 Emily.

"We'll stick posters on every tree," said Leo.

"The whole neighborhood will come,"
 said Emily.

"Where is it going to be?" asked Emily.

"Right here, in our backyard," said Leo.

"Why does everything always happen in your backyard?" asked Emily. "Couldn't it be in my backyard, for a change?"

"You don't have a pond," said Leo. "Every
zoo has a pond, for the seals, alligators,
and hippos."

"You don't have any seals, alligators, and
hippos," said Emily.

"But I have goldfish, frogs, and newts,"
said Leo.

"I doubt if anyone would want to pay ten cents to see goldfish, frogs, and newts," said Emily.

"I have my white rabbit," said Leo.

"I'll bring my black one," said Emily.

"It still doesn't look very much like a zoo,"
said Emily. "There aren't enough animals."
"You have to start somewhere," said Leo.
"When we have earned enough money, we'll
buy some more."

"A giraffe would be nice," said Emily.

"Or a kangaroo," said Leo.

"I like zebras," said Emily.

"But first of all we'll have to get a lion
and a monkey," said Leo.

"Let's make the posters," said Emily.

"The Grand Opening is on Sunday,"

said Leo.

On Sunday,
the whole neighborhood
stood at the gate.

· 14 ·

"Let's make a last-minute check before
we let them in," said Emily.
They went into the backyard.

"Where are the rabbits?" asked Emily.

"They tunneled themselves underground,"
said Leo.

"I can't see your goldfish, frogs, and newts,"
said Emily.

"They are at the bottom of the pond,"
said Leo.

"How are you going to explain that to the
neighbors?" asked Emily.

"It's natural," said Leo. "Bears hibernate in
tunnels. Seals, alligators, and hippos often
hide at the bottom of ponds."

"They'll want their ten cents back,"
  said Emily.
"There's nothing we can do!"
  said Leo.

Leo and Emily set up the box office
and opened the gate.
The whole neighborhood streamed in.
They stared into the pond and imagined
the seals, alligators, and hippos at the
bottom.

They tiptoed around the tunnel, not to wake
the hibernating bears inside.

"Is that all?" they asked.

"What more do you want?" asked Leo.

"A zoo!" said the neighbors. And they
started to leave.

A loud roar from Emily's backyard
made everybody jump.

"A lion!" shouted the people.

"A giraffe! A zebra! A monkey!

And a kangaroo!"

"We are saved!" said Leo.

"Where did they come from?" asked Emily.

"Not from very far," said Leo. "The zebra is wearing my mother's striped dress."

"The monkey looks like my mother's Halloween costume," said Emily.

"And what a funny kangaroo!" said Leo.

"It's wearing my grandma's clothespin apron," said Emily.

"The giraffe looks like my father on his stilts," said Leo.

"And the lion sounds like my father when he is angry," said Emily.

"Behind that fence they really look as
if they were in a cage," said Leo.
"And for a change, something is happening
in my backyard, too," said Emily.

"That was well worth the ten cents," said
   the neighbors.

"We told you," said Leo and Emily.

As soon as everyone was gone, the rabbits came out of their tunnel.

The fish, frogs, and newts swam to the surface of the pond.

"Time to feed the animals!" said Emily.

"Yes, it is!" said the lion, the giraffe, the zebra, the monkey, and the kangaroo.

"How did we do?" asked Leo.

"We are rich!" said Emily. "We
have enough to go to the real
zoo."

"I wish our parents and grandma
could come, too," said Leo.

"So do I," said Emily.

And their wish came true.